The Skeleton On Round Island

by Mary Hartwell Catherwood

I am to carry Mamselle Rosalin of Green Bay from Mackinac to Cheboygan that time, and it is the end of March, and the wind have turn from east to west in the morning. A man will go out with the wind in the east, to haul wood from Boblo, or cut a hole to fish, and by night he cannot get home—ice, it is rotten; it goes to pieces quick when the March wind turns.

I am not afraid for me—long, tall fellow then; eye that can see to Point aux Pins; I can lift more than any other man that goes in the boats to Green Bay or the Soo; can swim, run on snow-shoes, go without eating two, three days, and draw my belt in. Sometimes the ice-floes carry me miles, for they all go east down the lakes when they start, and I have landed the other side of Drummond. But when you have a woman with you—Oh God, yes, that is different.

The way of it is this: I have brought the mail from St. Ignace with my traino—you know the train-au-galise—the birch sledge with dogs. It is flat, and turn up at the front like a toboggan. And I have take the traino because it is not safe for a horse; the wind is in the west, and the strait bends and looks too sleek. Ice a couple of inches thick will bear up a man and dogs. But this old ice a foot thick, it is turning rotten. I have come from St. Ignace early in the afternoon, and the people crowd about to get their letters, and there is Mamselle Rosalin crying to go to Cheboygan, because her lady has arrive there sick, and has sent the letter a week ago. Her friends say:

"It is too late to go to-day, and the strait is dangerous."

She say: "I make a bundle and walk. I must go when my lady is sick and her husband the lieutenant is away, and she has need of me."

Mamselle's friends talk and she cry. She runs and makes a little bundle in the house and comes out ready to walk to Cheboygan. There is nobody can prevent her. Some island people are descend from noblesse of France. But none of them have travel like Mamselle Rosalin with the officer's wife to Indiana, to Chicago, to Detroit. She is like me, French.* The girls use to turn their heads to see me walk in to mass; but I never look grand as Mamselle Rosalin when she step out to that ice.

```
     * The old fellow would not own the Chippewa.
```

I have not a bit of sense; I forget maman and my brothers and sisters that depend on me. I run to Mamselle Rosalin, take off my cap, and bow from my head to my heel, like you do in the dance. I will take her to Cheboygan with my traino—Oh God, yes! And I laugh at the wet track the sledge make, and pat my dogs and tell them they are not tired. I wrap her up in the fur, and she thank me and tremble, and look me through with her big black eyes so that I am ready to go down in the strait.

The people on the shore hurrah, though some of them cry out to warn us.

"The ice is cracked from Mission Point to the hook of Round Island, Ignace Pelott!"

"I know that," I say. "Good-day, messieurs!"

The crack from Mission Point—under what you call Robinson's Folly—to the hook of Round Island always comes first in a breaking up; and I hold my breath in my teeth as I skurry the dogs across it. The ice grinds, the water follows the sledge. But the sun is so far down in the southwest, I think "The wind will grow colder. The real thaw will not come before to-morrow."

THE TRAIN-AU-GALISE

I am to steer betwixt the east side of Round Island and Boblo. When we come into the shadow of Boblo we are chill with damp, far worse than the clear sharp air that blows from Canada. I lope beside the traino, and not take my eyes off the course to Cheboygan, except that I see the islands look blue, and darkness stretching before its time. The sweat drop off my face, yet I feel that wind through my wool clothes, and am glad of the shelter between Boblo and Round Island, for the strait outside will be the worst.

There is an Indian burying-ground on open land above the beach on that side of Round Island. I look up when the thick woods are pass, for the sunset ought to show there. But what I see is a skeleton like it is sliding down hill from the graveyard to the beach. It does not move. The earth is wash from it, and it hangs staring at me.

I cannot tell how that make me feel! I laugh, for it is funny; but I am ashame, like my father is expose and Mamselle Rosalin can see him. If I do not cover him again I am disgrace. I think I will wait till some other day when I can get back from Cheboygan; for what will she say if I stop the traino when we have such a long journey, and it is so near night, and the strait almost ready to move? So I crack the whip, but something pull, pull! I cannot go on! I say to myself, "The ground is froze; how can I cover up that skeleton without any shovel, or even a hatchet to break the earth?"

But something pull, pull, so I am oblige to stop, and the dogs turn in without one word and drag the sledge up the beach of Bound Island.

"What is the matter?" says Mamselle Eosalin. She is out of the sledge as soon as it stops.

I not know what to answer, but tell her I have to cut a stick to mend my whip-handle. I think I will cut a stick and rake some earth over the skeleton to cover it, and come another day with a shovel and dig a new grave. The dogs lie down and pant, and she looks through me with her big eyes like she beg me to hurry.

But there is no danger she will see the skeleton. We both look back to Mackinac. The island have its hump up against the north, and the village in its lap around the bay, and the Mission eastward near the cliff; but all seem to be moving! We run along the beach of Bound Island, and then we see the channel between that and Boblo is moving too, and the ice is like wet loaf-sugar, grinding as it floats.

We hear some roars away off, like cannon when the Americans come to the island. My head swims. I cross myself and know why something pull, pull, to make me bring the traino to the beach, and I am oblige to that skeleton who slide down hill to warn me.

When we have seen Mackinac, we walk to the other side and look south and southeast towards Cheboygan.. All is the same. The ice is moving out of the strait.

"We are strand on this island!" says Mamselle Rosalin. "Oh, what shall we do?"

I tell her it is better to be prisoners on Bound Island than on a cake of ice in the strait, for I have tried the cake of ice and know.

"We will camp and build a fire in the cove opposite Mackinac," I say. "Maman and the children will see the light and feel sure we are safe."

"I have done wrong," says she. "If you lose your life on this journey, it is my fault."

Oh God, no! I tell her. She is not to blame for anything, and there is no danger. I have float many a time when the strait breaks up, and not save my hide so dry as it is now. We only have to stay on Round Island till we can get off.

"And how long will that be?" she ask.

I shrug my shoulders. There is no telling. Sometimes the strait clears very soon, sometimes not. Maybe two, three days.

Rosalin sit down on a stone.

I tell her we can make camp, and show signals to Mackinac, and when the ice permit, a boat will be sent.

She is crying, and I say her lady will be well. No use to go to Cheboygan anyhow, for it is a week since her lady sent for her. But she cry on, and I think she wish I leave her alone, so I say I will get wood. And I unharness the dogs, and run along the beach to cover that skeleton before dark. I look and cannot find him at all. Then I go up to the graveyard and look down. There is no skeleton anywhere. I have seen his skull and his ribs and his arms and legs, all sliding down hill. But he is gone!

The dusk close in upon the islands, and I not know what to think—cross myself, two, three times; and wish we had land on Boblo instead of Round Island, though there are wild beasts on both.

But there is no time to be scare at skeletons that slide down and disappear, for Mamselle Rosalin must have her camp and her place to sleep. Every man use to the bateaux have always his tinder-box, his knife, his tobacco, but I have more than that; I have leave Mackinac so quick I forget to take out the storekeeper's bacon that line the bottom of the sledge, and Mamselle Eosalin sit on it in the furs! We have plenty meat, and I sing like a voyageur while I build the fire. Drift, so dry in summer you can light it with a coal from your pipe, lay on the beach, but is now winter-soaked, and I make a fireplace of logs, and cut pine branches to help it.

It is all thick woods on Round Island, so close it tear you to pieces if you try to break through; only four-footed things can crawl there. When the fire is blazing up I take my knife and cut a tunnel like a little room, and pile plenty evergreen branches. This is to shelter Mamselle Rosalin, for the night is so raw she shiver. Our tent is the sky, darkness, and clouds. But I am happy. I unload the sledge. The bacon is wet. On long sticks the slices sizzle and sing while I toast them, and the dogs come close and blink by the fire, and lick their chops. Rosalin laugh and I laugh, for it smell like a good kitchen; and we sit and eat nothing but toasted meat— better than lye corn and tallow that you have when you go out with the boats. Then I feed the dogs, and she walk with me to the water edge, and we drink with our hands.

It is my house, when we sit on the fur by the fire. I am so light I want my fiddle. I wish it last like a dream that Mamselle Rosalin and me keep house together on Round Island. You not want to go to heaven when the one you think about all the time stays close by you.

But pretty soon I want to go to heaven quick. I think I jump in the lake if maman and the children had anybody but me. When I light my pipe she smile. Then her great big eyes look off towards Mackinac, and I turn and see the little far-away lights.

"They know we are on Round Island together," I say to cheer her, and she move to the edge of the fur. Then she say "Good-night," and get up and go to her tunnel-house in the bushes, and I jump up too, and spread the fur there for her. And I not get back to the fire before she make a door of all the branches I have cut, and is hid like a squirrel I feel I dance for joy because she is in my camp for me to guard. But what is that? It is a woman that cry out loud by herself! I understand now why she sit down so hopeless when we first land. I have not know much about women, but I understand how she feel. It is not her lady, or the dark, or the ice break up, or the cold. It is not Ignace Pelott. It is the name of being prison on Round Island with a man till the ice is out of the straits. She is so shame she want to die. I think I will kill myself. If Mamselle Rosalin cry out loud once more, I plunge in the lake—and then what become of maman and the children?

She is quieter; and I sit down and cannot smoke, and the dogs pity me. Old Sauvage lay his nose on my knee. I do not say a word to him, but I pat him, and we talk with our eyes, and the bright camp-fire shows each what the other is say.

"Old Sauvage," I tell him, "I am not good man like the priest. I have been out with the boats, and in Indian camps, and I not had in my life a chance to marry, because there are maman and the children. But you know, old Sauvage, how I have feel about Mamselle Rosalin, it is three years."

Old Sauvage hit his tail on the ground and answer he know.

"I have love her like a dog that not dare to lick her hand. And now she hate me because I am shut on Round Island with her while the ice goes out. I not good man, but it pretty tough to stand that." Old Sauvage hit his tail on the ground and say, "That so." I hear the water on the gravel like it sound when we find a place to drink;

then it is plenty company, but now it is lonesome. The water say to people on Mackinac, "Rosalin and Ignace Pelott, they are on Round Island." What make you proud, maybe, when you turn it and look at it the other way, make you sick. But I cannot walk the broken ice, and if I could, she would be lef alone with the dogs. I think I will build another camp.

But soon there is a shaking in the bushes, and Sauvage and his bledgemates bristle and stand up and show their teeth. Out comes Mamselle Eosalin with a scream to the other side of the fire.

I have nothing except my knife, and I take a chunk of burning wood and go into her house. Maybe I see some green eyes. I have handle vild-cat skin too much not to know that smell in the dark.

I take all the branches from Rosalin's house and pile them by the fire, and spread the fur robe on them. And I pull out red coals and put more logs on before I sit down away off between her and the spot where she hear that noise. If the graveyard was over us, I would expect to see that skeleton once more.

"What was it?" she whisper.

I tell her maybe a stray wolf.

"Wolves not eat people, mamselle, unless they hunt in a pack; and they run from fire. You know what M'sieu' Cable tell about wolves that chase him on the ice when he skate to Cheboygan? He come to great wide crack in ice, he so scare he jump it and skate right on! Then he look back, and see the wolves go in, head down, every wolf caught and drown in the crack. It is two days before he come home, and the east wind have blow to freeze that crack over—and there are all the wolf tails, stick up, froze stiff in a row! He bring them home with him—but los them on the way, though he show the knife that cut them off!"

"I have hear that," says Rosalin. "I think he lie."

"He say he take his out on a book," I tell her, but we both laugh, and she is curl down so close to the fire her cheeks turn rosy. For a camp-fire will heat the air all around until the world is like a big dark room; and we are shelter from the wind. I am glad she is begin to enjoy herself. And all the time I have a hand on my knife, and the cold chills down my back where that hungry vild-cat will set his claws if he jump on me; and I cannot turn around to face him because Rosalin thinks it is nothing but a cowardly wolf that sneak away. Old Sauvage is uneasy and come to me, his fangs all expose, but I drive him back and listen to the bushes behind me.

"Sing, M'sieu' Pelott," says Rosalin.

Oh God, yes! it is easy to sing with a vild-cat watch you on one side and a woman on the other!

"But I not know anything except boat songs."

"Sing boat songs."

So I sing like a bateau full of voyageurs, and the dark echo, and that vild-cat must be astonish. When you not care what become of you, and your head is light and your heart like a stone on the beach, you not mind vild-cats, but sing and laugh.

I cast my eye behin sometimes, and feel my knife. It make me smile to think what kind of creature come to my house in the wilderness, and I say to myself: "Hear my cat purr! This is the only time I will ever have a home of my own, and the only time the woman I want sit beside my fire."

Then I ask Rosalin to sing to me, and she sing "Malbrouck," like her father learn it in Kebec. She watch me, and I know her eyes have more danger for me than the vild-cat's. It ought to tear me to pieces if I forget maman and the children. It ought to be scare out the bushes to jump on a poor fool like me. But I not stop entertain it—Oh God, no! I say things that I never intend to say, like they are pull out of my mouth. When your heart has ache, sometimes it break up quick like the ice.

"There is Paul Pepin," I tell her. "He is a happy man; he not trouble himself with anybody at all. His father die; he let his mother take care of herself. He marry a wife, and get tired of her and turn her off with two children. The priest not able to scare him; he smoke and take his dram and enjoy life. If I was Paul Pepin I would not be torment."

"But you are not torment," says Rosalin. "Everybody speak well of you."

"Oh God, yes," I tell her; "but a man not live on the breath of his neighbors. I am thirty years old, and I have take care of my mother and brothers and sisters since I am fifteen. I not made so I can leave them, like Paul Pepin. He marry when he please. I not able to marry at all. It is not far I can go from the island. I cannot get rich. My work must be always the same."

"But why you want to marry?" says Rosalin, as if that surprise her. And I tell her it is because I have seen Rosalin of Green Bay; and she laugh. Then I think it is time for the vild-cat to jump. I am thirty years old, and have nothing but what I can make with the boats or my traino; the children are not grown; my mother depend on me; and I have propose to a woman, and she laugh at me!

But I not see, while we sing and talk, that the fire is burn lower, and old Sauvage has crept around the camp into the bushes.

That end all my courtship. I not use to it, and not have any business to court, anyhow. I drop my head on my breast, and it is like when I am little and the measle go in. Paul Pepin he take a woman by the chin and smack her on the lips. The women not laugh at him, he is so rough. I am as strong as he is, but I am afraid to hurt; I am oblige to take care of what need me. And I am tie to things I love—even the island—so that I cannot get away.

"I not want to marry," says Rosalin, and I see her shake her head at me. "I not think about it at all."

"Mamselle," I say to her, "you have not any inducement like I have, that torment you three years."

"How you know that?" she ask me. And then her face change from laughter, and she spring up from the blanket couch, and I think the camp go around and around me—all fur and eyes and claws and teeth—and I not know what I am doing, for the dogs are all over me—yell—yell—yell; and then I am stop stabbing, because the vild-cat has let go of Sauvage, and Sauvage has let go of the vild-cat, and I am looking at them and know they are both dead, and I cannot help him any more.

The Skeleton On Round Island

"'I THINK THE CAMP GO AROUND AND AROUND ME'"

You are confuse by such things where there is noise, and howling creatures sit up and put their noses in the air, like they call their mate back out of the dark. I am sick for my old dog. Then I am proud he has kill it, and wipe my knife on its fur, but feel ashame that I have not check him driving it into camp. And then Rosalin throw her arms around my neck and kiss me.

It is many years I have tell Rosalin she did that. But a woman will deny what she know to be the trut. I have tell her the courtship had end, and she begin it again herself, and keep it up till the boats take us off Round Island. The ice not run out so quick any more now like it did then. My wife say it is a long time we waited, but when I look back it seem the shortest time I ever live—only two days.

Oh God, yes, it is three years before I marry the woman that not want to marry at all; then my brothers and sisters can take care of themselves, and she help me take care of maman.

It is when my boy Gabriel come home from the war to die that I see the skeleton on Round Island again. I am again sure it is wash out, and I go ashore to bury it, and it disappear. Nobody but me see it. Then before Rosalin die I am out on the ice-boat, and it give me warning. I know what it mean; but you cannot always escape misfortune. I cross myself when I see it; but I find good luck that first time I land; and maybe I find good luck every time, after I have land.

The Skeleton On Round Island

The Skeleton On Round Island

The Skeleton On Round Island

The Skeleton On Round Island

The Skeleton On Round Island

The Skeleton On Round Island

Made in the USA
San Bernardino, CA
12 May 2014